HURLY-BURLY

MACBETH MAYHEM!

ROSS MONTGOMERY

With illustrations by **Mark Beech**

Barrington Stoke

To all the kids who are so well behaved,
who are SO good at always doing the
right thing ... that no one notices them

First published in 2022 in Great Britain by
Barrington Stoke Ltd
18 Walker Street, Edinburgh, EH3 7LP

www.barringtonstoke.co.uk

Text © 2022 Ross Montgomery
Illustrations © 2022 Mark Beech

The moral right of Ross Montgomery and Mark Beech to
be identified as the author and illustrator of this work has
been asserted in accordance with the Copyright, Designs and
Patents Act, 1988

A CIP catalogue record for this book is available
from the British Library upon request

ISBN: 978-1-80090-082-0

Printed by Hussar Books, Poland

CONTENTS

CHAPTER 1

Toil and Trouble

Three evil witches moved slowly around a smoking cauldron, wearing hooded robes and waving their hands in the air ...

Double double, toil and trouble;

Fire burn and caldron bubble.

Fillet of a fenny snake,

In the caldron boil and bake ...

Then one of the witches fell off the stage screaming. They'd tripped over their own robes – again.

"CUT!" yelled Mr Fortune, our headmaster. "Tomi, can you look where you're going, please? And, Leo, for the last time, stop picking your nose! We can see what you're doing under that hood, you know."

All the other children in the theatre groaned with frustration. I couldn't blame them. This rehearsal had been going on for hours!

"This is a disaster," said my best friend Rianna, who was sitting beside me. "The prize-giving assembly is in two days' time and it's still a total mess!"

"So?" I replied, shrugging. "Even if it does go wrong, everyone will be too excited about the prizes to care!"

The prize-giving assembly was the highlight of the school year. It took place on the last day of term. The theatre would be packed with every pupil, their parents and all the teachers. Mr Fortune would make a big speech and after that there would be a special performance to entertain the parents.

This year the drama club were going to perform some scenes from their latest play, William Shakespeare's *Macbeth*. That was why Tomi had just fallen off the stage, dressed as a witch.

At the end of the assembly came the best part of all – the prizes. There was a prize for top marks, a prize for best attendance, a prize for music …

And, of course, the prize for best behaviour. And we *all* knew who was going to win that one – me, Beth!

Everyone knew that I was the best-behaved girl in school. I never once handed in my homework late. I stayed behind after every lesson to help the teachers. I even cleaned the playground at break-time. That was why I had won the best-behaviour prize two years running – and this year I was on course to win it for the third time in a row!

I rubbed my hands with glee. I could almost taste that trophy! Rianna saw the look on my face and rolled her eyes.

"Honestly, Beth – you're obsessed with that stupid prize," she muttered.

"It's not just a prize," I said. "If I win three years in a row, that'll be a record for our school. I'll be famous!" I gazed at the stage. "I wonder if I'll be on the news …"

On the stage, poor Mr Fortune was looking even more stressed than normal. Our school, New Forest Academy, had had a lot of trouble lately. The theatre had caught fire during last year's school play, and this year's drama trip had been a total disaster when the ferry they were on capsized just off Dover!

I knew Mr Fortune was desperate to prove to the parents that the school had finally turned over a new leaf. I watched him scribble notes in his planner with a special red marker pen.

"Well, it's obvious that we've got a lot of work to do before the big day," Mr Fortune sighed. "Let me remind you all how important this assembly on Friday is – the school has to look its best for our visiting parents! I expect perfect behaviour, flawless uniforms ..."

Claire, one of the girls in my class, suddenly leapt to her feet.

"Don't worry, sir," she said. "I'll make sure your classroom is spotless, as always!"

I growled with annoyance. Claire was our classroom monitor. She was a complete clean freak – her desk was so polished you could lick soup off it. She even wiped Mr Fortune's whiteboard for him every day after school. What a goody-two-shoes!

But Claire wasn't the *only* one who was desperate to impress our headmaster. Another classmate, Duncan, stood up beside her.

"Don't worry about the parents, sir," he said. "My handmade banner is almost finished. The theatre will be looking its very best on Friday!"

I ground my teeth with irritation. Duncan was the best artist in the year. He had offered to make Mr Fortune a huge banner that would be unfurled above the stage at the start of the assembly. What a creep!

Mr Fortune couldn't have looked happier. "Thank you, Claire and Duncan," he said. "What a perfect example you two set your classmates!"

I gasped – I knew what Claire and Duncan were up to. They were trying to get their hands on my best-behaviour prize! I couldn't let them steal it from me right before the assembly. I leapt to my feet just as the bell rang for the end of the day.

"I'll stay behind and tidy up the theatre, sir!" I said as I shot Claire and Duncan a dirty look.

Mr Fortune smiled gratefully. "Thanks, Beth. I can always rely on you!"

He shoved his planner into his bag and raced out of the theatre. Everyone else followed, clearly wanting to get home after a long and boring rehearsal. Soon the only people left in the theatre were me and Rianna.

"What's got into you, Beth?" said Rianna, shaking her head. "You're too competitive! Prizes aren't everything, you know."

I gave her a playful push. "You can talk!" I said. "You're bound to win the drama prize after your performance in *Macbeth*!"

It was true – Rianna had stolen the show in the school play and she wasn't even the main character. Our classmate Frank had been great in the role of evil Macbeth – but it was Rianna who got the biggest round of applause at the end for playing Macbeth's best friend, Banquo.

Macbeth was about a brave Scottish warlord who was loved and respected by everyone. But after a battle one day, Macbeth and Banquo stumbled on three witches. The witches told Macbeth that he was destined to become King of Scotland.

At first Macbeth thought nothing of it – but he soon changed his mind when he thought of all the power he could have as ruler. With his wife, Lady Macbeth, he plotted to murder the king and take his place. He got away with it too – after the murder, Macbeth was crowned king and got everything he wanted!

But once the terrible deed was done, Macbeth was sure that he'd be found out – or that the other warlords would try to kill him and take his place. He started committing more and more awful crimes to cover up his first one. He even murdered his best friend, Banquo!

By the end of the play Macbeth had been driven mad with power. An army led by a warlord named Macduff came to overthrow him and finally brought peace back to Scotland.

It was a great play – gruesome and gory and scary. When Rianna came onstage as Banquo's ghost to haunt Macbeth, I thought the audience were going to wet themselves! She was going to perform the scene again for the parents during the prize-giving assembly. Maybe we needed to put some cling film over the seats …

Rianna shrugged. "I'm not bothered about winning the drama prize, to be honest. Things like that can go to your head if you're not careful." She glanced around the messy theatre. "Are you sure you're going to be able to tidy up all this on your own?"

"Of course!" I said. "That's what *best-behaved* pupils do, remember?"

Rianna shook her head again with a smile and raced off, leaving me alone in the dark theatre. It was really eerie when it was empty.

The stage was still decorated with spooky scenery from *Macbeth*, with a smoky backdrop and twisted branches.

But at least I finally had the stage to myself. In just two days' time I was going to be standing on this very spot, accepting the prize and creating a new school record. I had always known I was destined for great things – and now the school record was as good as mine. All my hard work would finally be worth it!

I already knew my victory speech word for word. The winner wasn't *supposed* to give a speech, but as it was such a special occasion I was sure Mr Fortune wouldn't mind.

I cleared my throat, stepped to the front of the stage and practised my final lines.

"And tomorrow," I said, "when the summer holidays begin, I know that I will have inspired all of you to work hard for your dreams!"

I bowed to the empty seats, imagining the cheers and applause ... and nearly leapt out of my skin.

Someone was *actually* clapping behind me.

It turned out I wasn't alone after all.

CHAPTER 2

Something Wicked
This Way Comes

I spun round to see who it was behind me. I realised that the stage wasn't as empty as I'd thought. Someone was skulking in the shadows beside the witches' cauldron, clapping me sarcastically.

"What a moving speech!" the person sniggered. "In fact, I'm so moved I might have to run to the toilets and be violently sick ..."

"Ugh – it's *you*, Robyn," I sighed, rolling my eyes.

Robyn was the naughtiest girl in school. No, forget that – Robyn was probably the naughtiest girl in history. It was clear Mr Fortune had given up trying to control her – I guessed letting her run riot was easier than battling with her every day.

"What are you doing here?" I asked, giving her a snooty look. "Shouldn't you be in after-school detention? *Again?*"

"Of course!" said Robyn. "I'm on my way there now. But there was something important I had to get my hands on first ..."

She held something up in the air and waggled it. It took me a few seconds to recognise what it was. But then I spotted the red marker pen clipped to the front. It was Mr Fortune's planner!

"H-how did you get that?" I gasped.

"I snatched it from his bag while he was
getting in his car!" said Robyn. "I thought I
could have some fun with it in detention.
After all, his most important notes are in
here – our end-of-year grades, the password
to his computer ... and the list of prizes for
the assembly!"

The hairs on the back of my neck stood on end. Robyn was right – the top-secret list of prize winners would be inside the planner. I couldn't let her mess with it right before the big day. She could change the list and ruin my chances of winning! I snatched the planner out of her hands.

"Oh no you don't!" I cried. "I'm going to put this back in Mr Fortune's office where it belongs!"

Robyn's eyes flashed with glee. "Of course – you'd never dream of taking a look inside the planner, would you, Beth? You're the most well-behaved girl in school!" She leaned forwards. "The question is ... are you well behaved *enough?*"

Robyn started laughing and didn't stop. I had no idea what she thought was so funny, but I wasn't going to waste any more time talking to her. I had a planner to return! I marched out of the theatre with my chin held high, Robyn's laughter echoing behind me.

I headed straight to Mr Fortune's office with the planner clutched safely to my chest. But when I got there, the office was already locked for the night!

There was only one place left where I could safely put the planner – Mr Fortune's classroom. He was our class teacher as well as being headmaster.

I could put the planner in his desk drawer for safekeeping and tomorrow morning I would tell him what I'd done. That was bound to get me in his good books – the best-behaviour prize had to be mine!

Even so, I could still hear Robyn's last words in my head. *Are you well behaved enough?* What did she mean? Had she seen the list of prize winners already? Was she trying to tell me that I hadn't won? Maybe I should check the list to make sure ...

I gasped and started marching towards the classroom. Of course I couldn't check the list! I'd never dream of doing something so badly behaved as looking inside a headmaster's planner! Even if it was just a little peek, just for a few seconds ...

I shook my head. What was wrong with me? It was Robyn, messing with my mind. I had to get rid of this planner as fast as possible!

I could already see Mr Fortune's classroom door ahead of me. All I had to do was put the planner in his desk, walk away and that was it. I didn't need to look at the list of prize winners – of course I'd won. I was the best-behaved girl in school!

But then ... if I *had* won, then it wasn't really cheating to look, was it? If anything, I *should* check the list. I'd need to see who came in second and third places so I could thank them properly in my victory speech. It would be rude of me not to!

I glanced behind me. The corridor was empty – I was completely alone. One quick look to see who I had beaten couldn't hurt, could it?

I sneaked behind a trophy cabinet and opened up the planner. My hands were shaking as I turned the pages. Was I really doing this? But before I could change my mind, the list of prize winners appeared right in front of me. I gasped – there was the best-behaviour prize at the top. And there was my name!

Best Behaviour

Third Place - Beth
Second Place - Duncan
First Place - Claire

I blinked. Hang on – third place? That couldn't be right. I must have read the list wrong.

I read it again – then again, and again. The list stayed the same. Was there something wrong with my eyes? I rubbed them a few times and looked at the list again.

There was nothing the matter with my eyes. The list said that Claire had won. But that was impossible! Was there some mistake? Maybe Mr Fortune had written the list in the wrong order. Or perhaps he had written the list in a special code and it was meant to be read backwards? Yes, that made sense! Didn't it?

But there was no point lying to myself. The truth came crashing down on top of me. I hadn't won the best-behaviour prize. I hadn't even come in second place. I was ... *THIRD!*

I leaned against the wall for support, my whole body shaking. I felt as if I was going to be sick. How had this happened? I had spent all year being perfect ... and it had been for nothing. The prize had been snatched from my hands at the very last second. My chance to beat the school record was gone!

The door suddenly opened beside me and someone stepped out of Mr Fortune's classroom. I pressed myself tight to the wall, not even daring to breathe.

It was clean-freak Claire, of course, finished tidying the classroom for the day. She closed the door behind her and squirted her favourite sanitiser over her hands, rubbing them together and humming under her breath. The sickly chemical smell of the sanitiser wafted through the air towards me. It was strong enough to make your eyes water. Oh, how I hated that smell!

Claire skipped away down the corridor, happy and carefree. She hadn't even noticed me. Suddenly I was seeing red. It was all her fault. *Claire* was the reason I was in third place! If it wasn't for her and that creep Duncan, the school record would be mine, all mine!

I gritted my teeth. I wouldn't let the two of them beat me when I was so close to glory. I wouldn't let all my hard work be for nothing. If they thought they could steal the prize from me – well, I was going to steal it right back!

The plan came to me in a heartbeat. I knew exactly what I had to do. It was wicked. It was brilliant. It was ... very, *very* badly behaved. Could I really do it?

I had no choice. This was my one and only chance for glory. It was time to show everyone what Beth was really made of!

I stepped out from behind the trophy cabinet and faced Mr Fortune's classroom door. Then I pulled the marker pen from its clip on the planner and twisted off the cap. The red tip glistened in the light of the corridor. There was no turning back now.

I held out the marker pen with shaking hands, pushed open the door and stepped inside the empty classroom ...

CHAPTER 3

Fair is Foul

The next morning, I acted as if nothing had happened. I strolled into school, holding open the doors for every teacher that I saw – just like normal. I was the same perfectly behaved girl as always.

But inside, my heart was pounding. I'd barely slept a wink the night before. I'd spent hours gazing up at my bedroom ceiling, thinking over what I'd done. What if my plan backfired? What if people found out what I'd done?!

But I arrived at Mr Fortune's classroom and could already tell that my plan had worked. A huge gang of kids were gathered outside the door, giggling while shoving each other to look inside. I pushed past them and found Rianna staring at the whiteboard with an open mouth. I gave her my best innocent look.

"Good heavens!" I exclaimed. "What on earth is the matter?"

Before Rianna could answer, Mr Fortune pushed his way past the crowd and into the classroom. He looked flustered and confused.

"What's going on?" he demanded. "Out of my way! Why is everyone ...?"

He turned to the whiteboard ... and his mouth fell open too. Normally the whiteboard was wiped clean each evening so it would be spotless for the first lesson in the morning. But it wasn't spotless today. Now it was filled with

huge red letters spelling out the words:
"Mr Fortune Guffs For England!"

Mr Fortune stared at the whiteboard in
disbelief.

"W-what is the meaning of this?" he cried.

Leo put up his hand. "Sir, I think it means that you're so good at guffing, you could represent the country at international level and—"

"I know what it means, you stupid boy!" bellowed Mr Fortune.

He grabbed a whiteboard eraser and tried to wipe off the words ... but it didn't work. They'd been written in permanent marker. There was no way of ever getting them off!

Mr Fortune turned round, glaring at us furiously.

"Who's responsible for this?" he demanded.

No one said anything – after all, no one had a clue who had written on the board.

I scratched my chin thoughtfully.

"A vandal must have broken in and done it last night, sir!" I said. "Claire, did you notice anything strange yesterday? After all, you were the last person in the classroom ..."

Everyone gasped and turned to Claire. It was true – Claire was *always* the last person in here, tidying up. And didn't the writing on the whiteboard look exactly like Claire's handwriting too? Of course it did – I'd taken all the books from her desk and carefully copied her handwriting a dozen times so the letters on the whiteboard would match hers. My plan was coming together perfectly!

Mr Fortune stared at Claire, his eyes widening.

"Let's get to the bottom of this," he said. "Claire, open your desk at once!"

Claire seemed too stunned to argue. She raced to her desk and opened it – after all, she thought she had nothing to hide. But the moment she lifted the lid, another gasp filled the room that was even louder than the first.

Lying on top of her books was Mr Fortune's planner ... along with his red marker pen! Mr Fortune looked at the whiteboard and down to Claire's desk, and put two and two together.

"Claire!" he cried. "What is my planner doing in your desk? Explain yourself!"

Claire had turned as pale as a ghost. "I ... I have no idea how that got there!"

But it sounded like a hopeless lie. Claire was so panicked, she was squeezing sanitiser over her shaking hands, cleaning them again and again to calm her nerves. She even *looked* guilty.

Mr Fortune needed no more convincing – he grabbed his planner and pointed to the classroom door.

"Straight to my office, immediately!" he bellowed at Claire. "After rehearsals, you and I are going to have a serious talk about your future at this school!"

Claire burst into tears and ran out of the room. Mr Fortune opened his planner and crossed something out angrily. I knew what that meant. He had just crossed Claire's name off the prize-winners list!

I made sure I looked as shocked as everyone else did, but inside I was jumping for joy. My plan had worked – I was one step closer to winning that prize. And best of all, no one had any idea it was me!

I looked down ... and felt a jolt of panic. There was something on my hands that I hadn't noticed before – a single spot of red ink. It must have been from writing the message last night! As quick as a flash, I pulled my shirt sleeves over my hands, just as Rianna turned to face me.

"Er … brrr!" I said, pretending to shiver. "Chilly in here, isn't it? My hands are freezing!"

Rianna frowned. "In July?" she said.

She had a point. I had to change the subject, fast.

"So … who would have thought that a goody-two-shoes like Claire would write something like that?" I said.

I pointed to the whiteboard, where Mr Fortune was trying to cover up the words "Mr Fortune Guffs For England!" with Post-it notes. Rianna frowned even harder, looking like someone trying to solve two crossword puzzles at once.

"Why would Claire write that?" she said. "Doesn't that seem a bit *odd* to you?"

I gulped. Rianna was smart – I had to come up with something before she worked out what had really happened.

"Well ... Claire always wanted to be cast as Lady Macbeth in the school play, didn't she?" I said. "Maybe she was getting revenge on Mr Fortune for casting her as Fleance instead!"

Rianna shook her head. "But why would she leave his planner in her desk? She could have taken it home so she wouldn't have been caught."

Luckily the bell rang at that very moment. I clapped Rianna on the back.

"Who knows?" I cried. "I'd better go – time for another assembly rehearsal!"

I raced out of the classroom before Rianna could ask any more questions. I breathed a sigh of relief. I had got away with it. There was no way that anyone would suspect me of framing Claire – that was why it was the perfect crime. I was the best-behaved girl in school! Now only one more person stood between me and my rightful prize.

I gazed over at Duncan. He was taking his special handmade banner out of his locker, showing it off to anyone who would look. It would be hanging in pride of place above the stage during the big prize-giving assembly tomorrow.

I let my mouth twist into an evil grin.

That's right, Duncan, I thought. *It's your turn next. Just you wait until the assembly starts tomorrow ...*

CHAPTER 4

Foul is Fair

It was Friday afternoon – time for the prize-giving assembly!

We'd had a final rehearsal that morning. After lunch, all the classes had filed into the theatre with their teachers, followed by the parents. Now the theatre was packed and buzzing with excitement. Our class were the last to arrive – it was clear that Mr Fortune wanted to make his grand entrance when everyone was seated and ready. He inspected our uniforms one final time to ensure they were perfect.

"Remember, children," said Mr Fortune, clearly very stressed. "We need to show that New Forest Academy is a changed school. This is our last chance – I mean, our *best* chance!" He turned to Duncan. "Duncan – is your banner in place?"

Duncan nodded. "Yes, sir! I gave it to the caretaker to hang up during lunch. It's rolled up above the stage, ready to be unfurled at the start of your speech!"

I grinned. Everyone had seen Duncan's banner in the final rehearsal this morning. It really was beautiful, spelling out "New Forest Academy Celebrates Excellence" in huge swirly letters.

Of course, no one was going to see *that* banner. They were going see the one that I had spent all night making. I'd swapped it at the very last second before the caretaker had hung it up. Both banners looked exactly the same when they were rolled up, so no one had any idea that I had swapped them.

Mr Fortune wiped his brow. "Well … it's time!" he said. "In we go, everyone!"

He took a deep breath and threw open the doors with a flourish. The audience turned to face us. The theatre had never looked more grand: the stage was still covered in branches from the school play, and bright sunshine was streaming in through every window.

Mr Fortune strode proudly down the central aisle to the stage. We followed behind him, taking our seats at the front just as we had practised in rehearsals.

I sat next to Rianna. She was dressed in her Banquo costume, ready for her special performance. Next to her sat Tomi, Leo and Taylor in their witches robes, and Frank in his Macbeth outfit.

"Beth, are you all right?" Rianna whispered, frowning at me. "You're sweating a lot."

"I'm fine!" I said. "Just ... excited, that's all!"

I was lying – I felt awful. Once again, I hadn't slept a wink all night – and not *just* because I'd been up late working on the banner. When I had finally gone to bed, I'd spent hours tossing and turning, thinking about Claire's face when she'd run out of the classroom in tears.

I didn't know why I felt so guilty – it wasn't as if Claire had been expelled! She'd just had her classroom monitor badge taken away and been given detention for a few days, that was all. It served her right for trying to steal my prize!

Besides, I couldn't let my face show my true feelings now. In just a few moments the final part of my plan would be revealed for all to see.

Mr Fortune stepped grandly onto the stage and cleared his throat.

"Ladies and gentlemen," he began. "Today, New Forest Academy celebrates excellence in all its forms! To start us off, we have something from Duncan. He has designed a special banner to welcome you all!"

Duncan jumped from his seat and raced to a rope at the side of the stage. The banner was still rolled tight above the stage, ready for its big reveal. One tug of the rope would open it up for all to see.

Mr Fortune raised his arms. "Without any further ado – welcome to this year's prize-giving assembly!"

Duncan pulled on the rope and the banner fell open. As expected, the audience gasped – but it wasn't a gasp of delight. It was a gasp of horror.

Mr Fortune blinked, no doubt wondering why everyone looked so shocked. He gazed up at the banner ... and a horrified gurgle escaped his throat. The banner didn't say "New

Forest Academy Celebrates Excellence". Instead
it said: "Mr Fortune Snogged a Dog!!!"

Mr Fortune's eyes bulged out of his head. "W-what's the meaning of this?!" he stuttered.

In the front row, Leo put up his hand. "I think it means that you like dogs so much—"

"I know what it means, you stupid boy!" Mr Fortune bellowed.

By now everyone in the theatre was muttering in shock and pointing at the banner. Mr Fortune turned to the audience, waving his hands desperately.

"Ladies and gentlemen, the message on that banner is a lie!" he cried. "I did no such thing! I don't even *like* dogs! If anything, I'm more of a cat person ..." Mr Fortune's eyes bulged even wider. "*But I'm not saying I snogged a cat!!*"

The theatre was in chaos now. All the parents were pointing, outraged – apart from the ones that were laughing. I tried to look as surprised as everyone else, but inside I was jumping double somersaults. My plan was working perfectly!

Mr Fortune spun round to Duncan, staring daggers of fury at him.

"Close it!" Mr Fortune screamed. "Close the banner!"

But Duncan was so confused and panicked that he was puffing away on his asthma inhaler, his face pale. Mr Fortune stormed across the stage and pulled the curtains shut, covering up the banner. From behind them I could just make out the sound of Mr Fortune bellowing at Duncan while he gasped on his asthma inhaler.

I rubbed my hands, delighted. I should have felt guilty ... but instead I felt triumphant. Duncan's chances of winning the best-behaviour prize had just gone up in flames. I had stolen it back from him. I had behaved worse than I'd ever behaved in my life ... and I had got away with it!

"Beth?"

I spun round. Rianna was staring at me.

"W-what's that on your hands?" she said, her voice hollow with shock.

I looked down – and gasped. The tell-tale mark of red ink was still on the back of my hand. How on earth was it still there?

"Oh, how weird!" I gasped. "Er ... I'm going to the toilet!"

I leapt from the front row and shot out of the theatre through a side door. My heart was thundering in my chest. I had to stop panicking – I couldn't give the game away, not when I was so close to winning the prize. Duncan and Claire were gone. The school record was mine, all mine!

Nothing could stop me now!

CHAPTER 5

Out, Damned Spot!

I charged into the girls' toilets and ran to the sinks, covering my hands in soap and scrubbing at the red mark.

I had no idea how the ink was still there – I must have cleaned my hands twenty times since I used Mr Fortune's marker pen. What on earth was permanent ink made from?

I closed my eyes. It was fine – I was just exhausted, that was all. I hadn't slept in two days! There was no way Rianna would link the mark on my hands with the message on the whiteboard. I was being paranoid. In a few more minutes I'd be standing at the front of the stage, delivering my victory speech.

I turned to the mirror and practised my most brilliant smile.

"And tomorrow," I recited, "when the summer holidays begin, I know that I will have inspired—"

I heard the door slam open. I almost jumped a metre into the air. Rianna was standing behind me in her Banquo costume. She had followed me into the toilets.

"R-Rianna!" I laughed nervously. "What are you doing here?"

But Rianna didn't laugh back. Her face was deadly serious. Her eyes were the saddest I had ever seen them.

"Beth," she said in a low voice, "I know what you did."

Her words sent a shiver up my spine. "I ... I beg your pardon?"

Rianna stepped towards me.

"I didn't want to believe it," she said. "I didn't want to think that you were capable of doing something so awful. But I saw the look on your face just now when Duncan was being shouted at. I know the truth.

"All the bad stuff that's happened over the last couple of days ... it was you. You replaced the banner above the stage. You wrote those words about Mr Fortune on the whiteboard. You framed Claire and Duncan so they wouldn't win that prize. How could you do it, Beth?"

My heart was pounding. I'd been found out!

"Th-that's ridiculous!" I said. "I'd never do anything so terrible! I'm the best-behaved girl in school! It must have been Robyn – this is exactly the sort of thing she'd do ..."

But Rianna shook her head. "You can't lie to me, Beth. I'm your best friend. I know how competitive you are. I know how much winning the prize and beating that record mean to you. But I never would have expected it to make you do something like *this*." Rianna folded her arms. "You have to tell Mr Fortune the truth. And if you don't ... I will."

I gasped with terror. I only had to take one look at Rianna's face to know that she wasn't bluffing. I had to make a run for it!

I looked around frantically, searching for any escape. But Rianna was standing between me and the exit. All the windows were locked. The only other door was the storage cupboard. I was trapped!

"Well, Beth?" said Rianna. "What are you going to do?"

I stared at Rianna … and suddenly my face screwed up with hate.

"I know what this is *really* about," I hissed. "You want that best-behaviour prize for yourself, don't you? You think you can take it from me at the last second! I should have known!"

Rianna looked horrified. "Beth, listen to yourself. Look at what you've become. This prize has turned you into a monster!"

But there was no stopping me now. I saw the key sticking out of the lock of the storage cupboard – and I knew what I had to do.

"No!" I cried. "You can't have it! That prize is mine, all mine!"

I threw open the cupboard door and shoved Rianna inside. She fell into a pile of cleaning supplies, and an avalanche of loo rolls tumbled on top of her. The last thing I saw before I slammed the door was Rianna's shocked face peeking up from a mound of white paper.

"Beth, what are you doing?!" she yelled. "Stop!"

I turned the key, then stumbled back to the sinks. I could hear Rianna pounding against the door with her fists, but it was no use. The door was locked.

"*Beth! Let me out!*" Rianna cried.

I shook my head. "N-not until I have my prize. I'll let you out after the assembly!"

I turned from the cupboard and fled, pretending that I couldn't hear Rianna's cries behind me. It was fine – I'd find some way to cover up what had happened. I'd tell Mr Fortune that Rianna was lying, or that it was all Robyn's fault. This was my only chance to win the prize and beat the school record. That was all that mattered!

But I gazed down at my hands and could see that they were trembling. The tell-tale spot of red ink was still there, proving my guilt. I hadn't just got rid of my rivals to win the prize – now I had even got rid of my best friend.

What had I done?

CHAPTER 6

Sleep No More

The next few minutes were a blur. I came back into the theatre and told everyone that Rianna was feeling sick, so I had taken her to the nurse's office. Mr Fortune was far too stressed about the banner to care and just told Frank and the others they'd have to perform another scene that didn't involve Banquo. I sat back down in the front row and the prize-giving assembly finally began.

Mr Fortune recited his end-of-year speech, blushing bright red. I didn't hear a word of what he was saying. I was thinking of Rianna, trapped inside that cupboard. Would she be OK in there? What if she was hurt?

I tried to stay calm, but I felt as if every eye in the theatre was staring straight at me. The twisted branches onstage almost seem to loom towards me like a hundred pointing fingers ...

I shook my head. It wasn't real – I was just tired! In a few minutes I was going to step out on that stage and accept my prize. That was all that mattered!

Mr Fortune finished his speech to a round of applause. He breathed a sigh of relief – no doubt because finally things were going to plan!

"And now," he announced, "before we hand out the prizes, we're going to have a scene from this year's standout production of *Macbeth*!"

It was just Frank who made his way onstage. Clearly, without Rianna, they couldn't do the scene with the witches any more. I caught sight of Rianna's empty seat beside me and felt another pang of guilt. She should have been here, wowing the audience with her amazing acting skills, not locked inside a cupboard ...

Frank didn't seem at all worried by the last-minute change in scene. He turned to face everyone, took a deep breath and let his words ring out through the theatre:

> *Methought I heard a voice cry,*
>
> *"Sleep no more!*
>
> *Macbeth does murder sleep ..."*

The words filled me with horror. I remembered this speech from the play. After Macbeth has committed his terrible crimes, he can no longer sleep – just like me! My heart began to pound. Had Frank chosen this speech for a reason? Was he trying to send me a message? Did he know what I'd done? I could swear Frank was even looking right at me while he said the words ... Or maybe it was just a trick of the light? The sun streaming through the windows was now so bright I could barely see. The heat in here was getting unbearable too.

I began to sweat. What if Frank *did* know the truth? Was I going to have to deal with him too, like I had dealt with Rianna? Oh, when would this nightmare end?

Frank finished his speech and returned to his seat as the audience applauded. Mr Fortune looked delighted – the assembly was finally going well! He opened his planner and cleared his throat.

"And now the moment we've all been waiting for – the prizes!" he said. "We will start with the award for best behaviour. Normally I would begin by announcing the runners-up, but ... er ... that's not going to happen this year."

Mr Fortune glanced at Claire and Duncan, who were slumped miserably in the front row. I felt another pang of guilt in my stomach – they both looked so devastated. They must have been gutted to lose out on the prize after how hard they had both worked ...

I clenched my fists – *no!* I had to stop thinking like this. It was just the lack of sleep making me nervous, that was all. I couldn't look guilty now. In a few moments all eyes would be on me – I had to stroll onto that stage as if I owned it!

"Without any further ado," said Mr Fortune, "the winner of the best-behaviour prize is ... Beth!"

Everyone clapped. I gasped, pretending to be surprised, and marched onto the stage, bowing grandly. This was the moment I'd been waiting for: setting a new school record in front of all the teachers and parents! I strode towards Mr Fortune and shook his hand.

"Thank you, Mr Fortune!" I said. "If you don't mind, I happen to have a few words to mark this very special occasion."

Mr Fortune frowned. "We don't have time for—"

I ignored him and stepped to the front of the stage. I had practised my speech hundreds of times by now – I was going to ace this. I took a deep breath and began.

"It's such an honour to receive this award a record *three times*!" I said, my voice echoing around the theatre. "It's a perfect opportunity for me to reflect on all the terrible things I've done … er … I mean, all the wonderful things I've achieved!"

The audience chuckled at my mistake. But I was confused – why had I just said that? It must have been the sunlight in my eyes, putting me off – it felt like being trapped under a searchlight. It really was roasting hot in here.

"I … I couldn't have done this without the help and support of all the teachers," I said. "I'd never be standing here if it wasn't for their Claire and attention – I mean, their *care* and attention! I wouldn't be accepting this award from Mr Banner … I mean, Mr Rianna! I … I mean …"

People in the audience were muttering to one another now – something was clearly wrong with me. My hands were shaking – I couldn't focus.

From the corner of my eye I could make out the stage scenery shifting and swaying as if the trees were closing in on me. All I could think about was Rianna's face as I slammed the cupboard door, Duncan's face as he saw my banner, Claire's face as she ran out of the classroom in tears ...

This was a nightmare. I had to get offstage, fast! I skipped straight to the final line of my speech.

"And tomorrow ..."

I stopped. There was a sudden smell in the air – something that I had only just noticed in the last few seconds. A smell that almost made my eyes water. It was the sickly chemical smell of ... hand sanitiser.

I looked down at the front row and gasped. There was Claire, staring at me with a look of absolute hate ... and squeezing that awful, awful sanitiser into her hands, rubbing them over and over. A chill shot up my spine. Did Claire know what I had done? Did she know I was guilty?

I tried to keep going, my voice shaking.

"And tomorrow ..."

That was when I heard the *hiss* of an asthma inhaler. I looked to the seat beside Claire – and there was Duncan, glaring at me with rage as he puffed away on his inhaler. Did he know the truth too? Did *everyone* know the truth?! My voice stammered and shook as I tried to finish my speech.

"And tomorrow ..."

The audience were shifting in their seats now, trying to work out what was wrong with me. My speech was falling apart. Mr Fortune ran over and tried to usher me offstage as fast as possible.

"Er ... thank you, Beth!" he cried. "Now, on with the other prizes ..."

WHAM!

The sound of a slamming door filled the theatre. Everyone turned to face the side door – and gasped with surprise.

I could hardly bring myself to look – but I knew I had to. I had a horrible feeling that I knew exactly who would be standing there when I did ...

I turned to look with dread ... and there, standing in the doorway, was Rianna. She was still in her Banquo costume, covered from head to toe in long white strands of toilet paper. She

looked just like Banquo's ghost ... and her finger
was pointed straight at me.

I couldn't take it any more. I finally
snapped.

"NOOOOOOOOOOOOOOOOOOOO!" I screamed.

I fell to my knees in front of the shocked
audience.

"It was me – I did it!" I confessed. "*I* wrote 'Mr Fortune Guffs For England' on the whiteboard! *I* made the banner that said he snogged a dog! *I* locked Rianna in the toilets! It was me, all me!"

Everyone gasped. Mr Fortune looked as if he was about to have a heart attack – but there was no stopping me now.

"I did it all!" I went on. "I wanted to get rid of Claire and Duncan so I could win the best-behaviour prize and beat that stupid school record! That's right – I BROKE THE RULES!"

By now everyone in the audience was on their feet, shouting with confusion and disbelief. I raised my arms and bellowed as loudly as I could.

"Punish me!" I cried. "Suspend me! Expel me! Put me in detention for the rest of my life! But for heaven's sake, for all that is good and holy ... *just – let – me – sleep!*"

The stage was spinning around me.
But I had done it. The truth was out. I was
free – I was finally, finally free!

With a gurgle, I fell off the stage and fainted.

CHAPTER 7

What's Done is Done

It was one week later. Term was over, the summer holidays had begun and the sun was high in the sky. The corridors of New Forest Academy would be empty for six long and blissful weeks.

But not *completely* empty.

"Beth! Stop dawdling!"

I turned around. Mr Fortune was standing beside his desk, tapping his foot.

"There's no point staring out the window," he said. "You've still got another ninety thousand lines to do!"

I groaned. This was my punishment for everything I had done – I had to sit in Mr Fortune's classroom every day of the holidays until I had written "I must not tell lies about my headmaster" a hundred thousand times. It was going to take me all summer to do it!

But I deserved it. I really should have been expelled for what I'd done. Instead, to my surprise, Rianna and Claire and Duncan had stood up for me. They asked Mr Fortune not to expel me and said that I just needed to be taught a lesson.

Mr Fortune had agreed, on the condition that he could oversee my punishment himself. He was clearly getting his own back on me for ruining his chance to impress the parents at the prize-giving assembly.

"Right!" said Mr Fortune. "My new whiteboard is about to arrive. I'll have to let the delivery people in." He glared at me. "No moving from that chair until I get back!"

I nodded. From now on I really was going to be on my best behaviour. And not so I'd win prizes – now it was because I didn't want to hurt people ever again.

However, there was *one* more rule I had to break.

Mr Fortune marched out of the room and left me alone. A few seconds later, a familiar face appeared at the window.

"Finally!" said Robyn. "I thought he'd never leave."

Robyn had agreed to help me with my final rule-breaking – maybe it was because she felt bad for me. It turned out that it was Robyn who had let Rianna out of the storage cupboard during the assembly – she'd been wandering the school by herself, as usual, and heard Rianna's cries for help. I knew I should never have got involved with the naughtiest girl in school! But knowing someone like Robyn did have its advantages.

"Well, here they are," Robyn said. "It wasn't easy, getting all three of them over the school fence …"

I looked behind her – and felt a tremble in my heart. Three more familiar faces were standing in the playground behind Robyn. It was Claire and Duncan … and Rianna.

It was the first time I'd seen them since the last day of term – when they had spoken up for me in front of Mr Fortune. None of them had said a word to me since – and who could blame them? After everything I'd done, they should never want to see me again.

"Well?" said Rianna, folding her arms.
"What is it, Beth? Why did you bring us here?"

There was a heavy silence. I blushed with shame.

"I wanted to say how sorry I am," I began. "Claire, Duncan – what I did to you both was awful. The fact that you both stood up for me … it's clear that you deserved that best-behaviour prize more than me."

Mr Fortune had made Claire and Duncan both joint winners of the best-behaviour prize to make up for what had happened.

"It's fine," said Claire. "To be honest, the way you confessed to everything onstage and then passed out was kind of funny."

"I thought Mr Fortune was going to explode!" said Duncan.

I turned to Rianna and my eyes filled with tears. This was going to be the hardest apology of all.

"Rianna, I don't even know where to begin," I said. "Everything you said was right. I've learned an important lesson about myself.

I thought I was well behaved, but it turns out I have a bit of a mean side. I'm going to make sure nothing like that ever happens again. Do you think you can ever forgive me?"

Rianna gave me a pained look. "Forgive you?" she said. "Beth, you could have really hurt me!"

I nodded, feeling nothing but shame. It was so terrible.

"But I can see you're trying to make up for it," said Rianna. "So, for what it's worth, I don't think you're *completely* bad."

I looked up, blinking through my tears. "And can we ever be friends again?" I asked.

"Maybe ... I don't know," she sighed. "I'm going to need some time."

I nodded. "Of course – I'll wait as long as you need!"

Robyn nudged the others. "Right, we'd better go. I can see Mr Fortune coming back along the corridor!"

Rianna smiled at me. "Good luck with your punishment. I'll see you around, Beth."

With that, the four of them walked off into the sunset – Rianna, Robyn, Claire and Duncan. I watched my best friend leave, my heart glowing. I was so sad to have lost Rianna's trust – so sad to have hurt her. But I took hope from her words. There was a chance that we could be friends again – a chance that one day I could set everything right. And that was worth all the punishment in the world.

Mr Fortune stormed back into the room.

"I heard voices in here!" he said suspiciously. "If I find out you were breaking another rule ..."

I shook my head. "No, sir. My rule-breaking days are over!"

Mr Fortune gave me a careful look. "Glad to hear it! I can punish you further if that's what it takes. A hundred thousand lines is nothing – the school record is two hundred thousand lines!"

My pencil froze on the paper. I looked up.

"Did you just say ... 'school record'?" I asked quietly.

"Yes!" said Mr Fortune. "Mark my words, one more bad deed from you and I'll triple your punishment. You'll go down in the history books – the worst-behaved child in New Forest Academy! Now, where did I put my good tie? The school inspectors are on their way and I want to make sure I make a good impression on them ..."

Mr Fortune kept talking, but I wasn't really listening. All I could hear were those words going round and round in my head ...

The worst-behaved child in New Forest Academy.

You know, I quite liked the sound of that …